CORONA VIRUS

CORONA VIRUS

The Truth Is Known

Dr. François Adja Assemien

Copyright © Dr. François Adja Assemien.

All rights reserved. No part of this book may be reproduced in any form or by any electronic or mechanical means, including information storage and retrieval systems, without permission in writing from the publisher, except by reviewers, who may quote brief passages in a review.

ISBN: 978-1-63649-214-8 (Paperback Edition)
ISBN: 978-1-63649-215-5 (Hardcover Edition)
ISBN: 978-1-63649-213-1 (E-book Edition)

Book Ordering Information

Phone Number: 315 288-7939 ext. 1000 or 347-901-4920
Email: info@globalsummithouse.com
Global Summit House
www.globalsummithouse.com

Printed in the United States of America

CONTENTS

Introduction xiii

FIRST PART
THE PHILOSOPHICAL ORIGIN OF CORONA VIRUS

Hegemonism: Will To Power, Will To Domination 3
Eugenism 7
Scientism And Scientific Curiosity 11
Racism And Anthropology 13

SECOND PART
THE SOCIO-POLITICAL ORIGIN OF CORONA VIRUS

Slavery 19
Colonialism-Neocolonialism 21
Globalization - Colonization 23
The Terrorism Of Globalizing Powers 27
Nature And Value Of Humanity 29
Conclusion 33
Book Summary 35
Author Biography 37

Who rules the world?

Where is the world going to?
Does life have a value?

By THE SAME AUTHOR

- The African Rebels, novel, 2016
- The Golden Rules of Happiness, Success, Personal Health and Salvation, Essay, Edilivre, 2016
- Introduction to Philocure, essay, Edilivre, 2016
- Moral and spiritual education, essay, Edilivre, 2016
- Forbidden Africa, novel, Edilivre, 2019
- The Way of Living in America, guide, Edilivre, 2019
- The Current slavery in Africa, essay, Global Summit House, 2020
- The World is worth nothing, essay, Edilivre, 2019
- Côte d'Ivoire hurts, essay, Edilivre, 2019
- Thomas Sankara like Thomas More and Socrates, essay, Ouagadougou, 2020
- African Consciousness, essay, Edilivre, 2016
- Afrocratism, essay, 2012
- Ahikaba, novel, Mary Bro Foundation, London, 2018
- Electoral code, novel, EBAV Stars, 1995
- Portrait of the good and the bad voter, the good and the bad candidate, essay, 2000
- Côte d'Ivoire against its foreigners, essay, Black Stars, 2002
- Political Thought to Save Côte d'Ivoire, essay, Afro-Star, 2003

I DEDICATE THIS BOOK

To

Jean-Dominique Michel
Didier Raoult
Arikana Chihombori-Quoa
Ngolo Tatua
Nathalie Yamb
Claire Newman (Gabonese)
Aminata Traore
Mamoushka Under the Baobab
Fatou Diom e
Samuel Eto 'o
Didier Drogba
Elianne Nkolo
Ebene Bouanay (Marie-Gabrielle Tecka)
Mwazulu Diyabanza
Lise Manzambi
Zack Mwekassa
Jerôme Munyangi (Congolese Doctor-researcher)
Andry Rajoelina (President of Madagascar)
Dr Vangu Lutete (Congolese Doctor-researcher)
Ema krusi

INTRODUCTION

Is the disease called Covid-19 a mystery? Is this the biggest mystery these days? Many people are dying every day around the world. They are said to be killed by the corona virus. This phenomenon is currently the greatest danger or the worst enemy of humanity. It is said to be a biological weapon (like Ebola, AIDS and others) being tested by the West. Why? With what intentions? For what objectives? President Emmanuel Macron says his country, France, is at war. He says that France is attacked by an invisible enemy (mystery). He thus speaks of covid-19 which kills French people. What grotesque hypocrisy! Those who rule the world (the powerful) are not telling the truth about covid-19 which is their evil creation. They lie to us and hide the truth about this general and catastrophic evil from us. They carefully hide from us its exact, real origin and nature. It is their state secret. And they have a clear conscience. They are free, in peace, in security, in good health, not at all worried, threatened. They are free from all suspicion, accusation, guilt, indictment, conviction and sanction. They play the innocent, the saints, the divine, the saviors, the philanthropists and the virtuous ascetics. So they are both arsonists and firefighters. What a plot! What a combination! What machiavellianism!

It increases our intellectual, scientific or philosophical curiosity. Everywhere is panic, psychosis, stampede, paranoia. People are dying by the hundreds, by the thousands, or maybe by the millions here and there. It is the massacre, the holocaust and the universal genocide. Everyone is confined to the house. Streets, public places and workplaces are deserted. No more work, no more travel, no more happiness, no more cheerfulness, no more pleasure, no more health, no more security, no more peace, no more contact or trust between men. no more food in every sense of the word. State of siege and curfew everywhere. What are the military, police and gendarmes doing at night in the world? Do they create security or insecurity? Are they fighting the poison of the corona virus or, on the contrary, are they spreading it everywhere to the great misfortune of populations ignorant, manipulated, mystified, indoctrinated, sheep and kept very far from the secret of corona virus (the greatest state secret all time)? Total and absolute mystery!

We thus see the end of the world approaching very fast. Yes, the end of the human world is looming on the horizon through the fault, wickedness and cruelty of the powerful and rulers of our planet. And each person is more or less preparing to die a violent death, by poisoning, imposed on all. What have we done to deserve such a collective fate wanted and decided by leaders, influential men, politicians, ideologists, bourgeois, bloodthirsty capitalists, satanics? Who will be able to save humanity from this genocide, from the horrors of this "New World Order", from this cowardly, sly and discreet war of globalization which wants to exterminate humans?

We learn that these executioners want to depopulate the earth, reduce the world population drastically, dominate the world (which they have always dominated), get richer, better take advantage of the goods and riches of the earth, most of which are concentrated in Africa. Such is the genocidal plot. This imperialist and capitalist action of depopulation of the earth mainly aims to create a kind of global village (unification of all countries), to exterminate Africans sitting on natural treasures which they themselves do not benefit from being possessed by Europeans, to control all humans, who will survive the genocide in progress, by electronic chips that they will put in their blood through compulsory vaccinations. So the globalizers will make most people sick, turn them into zombies, and pretend to cure them by selling them drugs and vaccines (business) that will kill them. For globalizers, it is a question of becoming very rich, very prosperous, and of living their earthly paradise by reigning over sheep-men and robots.

FIRST PART

THE PHILOSOPHICAL ORIGIN OF CORONA VIRUS

1

HEGEMONISM: WILL TO POWER, WILL TO DOMINATION

Hegemonism is one of the origins of covid-19. What is hegemonism? It is the tendency to want to dominate others. We know, for example, that the West is used to dominating Africans, to maintaining a balance of power, from dominator to dominated, from master to slave with other peoples.

There are many possibilities, means or methods by which one people can exercise domination over another. Among these means, there are morals, religion, science, ideology, philosophy, technology etc. For Nietzsche, the class of the weak, the sick, the slaves, the reprobates, the decadents uses ascetic morality (the theory of Good and Evil as a plot or weapon) to weaken, alienate, subdue, overthrow and defeat the class of the strong, the masters, the powerful, the dominant. The class of the miserable, the despicable, the ashamed thus overturns the balance of power, from dominator to dominated, in its favor. The slave thus finds his freedom, his salvation and power. For Karl Marx, the rich capitalists, the bourgeois exploiters, use religion as opium to lull the conscience of the popular and working masses. Religion constitutes a sedative, an alienating sedative which promotes and facilitates the exploitation, oppression, submission and domination of man by man. The current global health crisis is a matter of the West's desire for domination. Mafia, cynical political leaders, influential, powerful businessmen of the earth are using science and technology to assert their will to dominate, control and destroy mankind. Science is neither neutral nor disinterested. It is a formidable and terrifying weapon. It allows you to do everything (both good and bad). It all depends on the will and intentions of its manipulator or user. Chemistry, biology and physics enhance the demonic power, the nuisance capacity of Westerners and Asians. Ordinary, minor terrorism uses conventional weapons of mass destruction produced by science. And current, major terrorism uses the corona virus created by Western and Asian scientists to massacre the peoples to be dominated, to be exterminated. The will to power and domination has generated scientific knowledge, exact or experimental science (biology, chemistry, physics).

Indeed, science has provided the peoples of the West and Asia with terrifying weapons of mass destruction. It has increased their capacity for evil, for infinite nuisance. For example, the atomic bomb, the nuclear weapon and the corona virus. All the wars which have taken place (or which are in progress) in the world are wars of domination and interest (geopolitical, geo-economic, geo-strategic, geo-spiritual, geo-cultural interest...). And they are always done with more and more powerful, sophisticated and efficient weapons. The corona virus, like Ebola and AIDS, is one such weapon that sows widespread terror, panic, psychosis, desolation and paranoia. The corona virus manufactured by Chinese, French and others is indeed the fruit of the will to power, domination and genocidal ambitions of these predators.

2

EUGENISM

Another origin or cause of corona virus is eugenics. The creators of corona virus and the globalizers aim to select humans and peoples. They don't want to see all men live. The world, as it is, bothers and annoys them. The earth is populated with different peoples that they find unworthy or cumbersome to live in, humans that they hate. For example, the old and certain people they do not like and which they want to make disappear. There are, in particular, Blacks and Africans. This attitude is characteristic of Western racists, slavers, colonialists and imperialists. Adolf Hitler and Nazists practiced eugenics (antisemitism). They tried to exterminate the Jews. It is the holocaust. Thus Western imperialism is Western ethnocentrism, Europeocentrism, that is to say racism, contempt for races, peoples enslaved, colonized, dominated by the West (Europe, America). Eugenics causes people to underestimate, to inferior, to discriminate against those who are different from them. Thinkers, philosophers and writers like Voltaire, Gobineau, Hegel, Levi-Bruhl, have strived to demonstrate and prove that Blacks, Africans, are not men, that they are animals, things, objects devoid of soul, Reason, intelligence, culture and civilization. So they deserve to be sold, mistreated, massacred, enslaved, colonized. This is the ideology or the mentality of the West which explains the suffering and the endless ordeal of Blacks and Africans. Occidentalocentrism is racism, eugenics, elitism, delusional collective narcissism. It is ultimately the **solipsism** (Westerners think wrongly that they are the only true humans on earth, the only ones to exist in the world as humans).

Hitler (disciple and hero of Nietzsche) and his followers valued the Aryan people at the expense of other peoples of the earth they despised and hated. They treated the French as dwarfs and scoundrels who have no right to live in this world. The Aryan was considered by them as the model, the human prototype which was to impose itself on all the other peoples of the world. The Aryan is the type of man chosen by God. He is the master. He is very tall, barbaric, violent, cruel. He is a bird of prey (predator, destroyer, killer), a blond beast, a triumphant warrior. In front of him are the decadent, the weak, the sick, the stunted, the dwarves, the slaves, the little ones. Nietzsche thus praises the Pre-Aryans, his German ancestors. He glorifies them. He condemns the Jews and their morality of resentment inspired by the spirit of vengeance, hatred and jealousy (see "The Genealogy of Morals" and "Beyond Good and Evil"). Nietzsche distinguishes the morality or the thought of the masters, the aristocrats, the warriors, the Aryan victors of the priestly, Christian morality, the weak, the ascetic priests, the decadents, the reprobates, the suffering, the slaves, the Jews. He is violently opposed to this because for him it is the cause of the world's decadence. It is nihilism (see "European nihilism") and the negation of the will to live. It is a bitter war between Aryans and Jews. The Jews, on the other hand, claim to be the superior people, the chosen people of God. Let's say that these two groups, Jews and Aryans, are equally sick, ill-minded, eugenicists, racists, imperialists. Let us remember that corona virus came out of this Nazi and Jewish ideology or dangerous school of thought.

3

SCIENTISM AND SCIENTIFIC CURIOSITY

Corona virus, as a deadly phenomenon, is the result of scientific development. It arises from intellectual, scientific curiosity. Man needs to know and understand beings, things, to discover the forces and laws of nature, of universe, of the world. Indeed, ignorance, illusion, prejudices and dogmas of all kinds are harmful to man. These are dreadful evils. So man makes it his duty to struggle to know and demystify beings, things. Fear of the unknown and curiosity lead man to science. "Science hence law, law hence forecast, forecast hence action", said Auguste Comte. Man is endowed with Reason, intelligence and consciousness. He is a thinking being. "I think therefore I am" (Cogito ergo sum), said René Descartes. The human mind is constantly thinking, questioning and functioning. It never sleeps. It is dynamic. Thus it discovers the truth about beings and things. It establishes cause and effect relationships between natural, human and social phenomena (laws). It explains the phenomena in relation to each other by relating them to their causes. Science is deterministic or it is not. It is effective because it allows us to act on the world, to transform it and to dominate it. This is why René Descartes says that science and technology (his daughter) will make man as master and owner of nature.

The combination of science and technique (technology) gives man formidable power or might. Thanks to this, man creates means (machines and methods) to improve his life, defend himself and dominate others. The law of the weight (physical) discovered by Isaac Newton made it possible to send machines in the air space (planes, rockets, missiles). This facilitates air transport. The law of the water pressure discovered by Archimedes (eureka) makes it possible to circulate on the water with boats. Knowledge of the atom makes it possible to manufacture the atomic bomb. Knowledge of the properties of uranium enables the creation of terrifying nuclear weapons and electricity. Thus, knowledge of bacteria, viruses and microbes makes it possible to treat patients, to give them good health, but also to manufacture deadly poisons, weapons of mass destruction such as the corona virus, Ebola, AIDS, Plague ... Absolute faith in science (scientism) is the best and the worst thing. The best of things when one thinks of the indisputable benefits of science and the worst of things when one thinks of the very many indisputable and real misdeeds of science-technology that humanity is currently facing. Medium does not imply right. Science without conscience is fatal to man. It causes catastrophe and destruction of humanity. This is the case with corona virus fabricated from scratch by Western and Asian scientists and exploited as a chemical-physical - biological weapon by demons, mafiosi, terrorists and capitalist globalizers who want to depopulate the earth, create a new world order, a new planetary civilization to their liking and get richer (business).

4

RACISM AND ANTHROPOLOGY

Racism is the attitude or e state of mind of an individual, of a race, a people who despises and degrades another race or another people. This is at the origin of corona virus, of the bio-chemico -physical war that is currently being waged against Africans and other peoples by Westerners and Asians. During Apartheid era, in South Africa, racist white scientists (Mr Doctor of Death) were making poisons or vaccines used against Blacks. They sought to exterminate the Blacks, the legitimate owners of South African lands. They sterilized black women and poisoned children. Thus were born deadly dangers like Ebola, AIDS and others. And now it's time for corona virus that is ravaging Africa. Racist whites want an Africa without Africans which will be their paradise. It came out of the mouth of Mr. John Vorster, ex Prime Minister and ex President of South Africa. They want to tear Africa away from Africans by taking their lives. To do this, they have created all kinds of strategies, means, pretexts and ideologies.

So they accuse Africans of having too many children. They say the Africans will invade them later and deprive them of their well-being, their security and destroy their culture. They claim that Africans are and will be too heavy as social, economic and financial burden for them, that it will put their lives in danger and cause their misfortune, their misery. They believe that Africans will be a formidable force and power which will crush them on all levels, which they will not be able to contain, control, dominate, support. They believe Africans will wipe them off the earth. Thus Africa, which is their true paradise on earth, is presented in their deceptive collective imagination as their future hell, as their future rival or mortal enemy. So they decided to wage a preventive war on it as they usually do with other peoples (Iraq, Libya...). That is their favorite alibi to machiavellianly legitimize their crimes and their multiple crimes against black humanity. This results in military occupation, genocide, shameless looting and cynical exploitation of other countries.

Thus racism is characterized by unjustified fear, jealousy, envy, hatred, contempt, lies, violence, dishonesty, wickedness, barbarism, unjust war, gratuitous, far-fetched accusation, and unjust condemnation of others. It's the policy of saying, "Get out of here so I can get on with it". Racism really means: I'm afraid of you. You are superior to me. You are too rich. You are too powerful. I want you. I am jealous of you. I hate you. I kill you and I take your place, your goods, your riches. I seek my happiness, my security, my salvation at your expense. Mr Emmanuel Macron, President of France, said that the problem of Africa is civilizational, that Africans are having too many children and that giving billions of Euros to Africans cannot be used for their development. Let us ask this question. Is it

France that nourishes and develops Africa or is it rather the reverse? Let's read the famous **Colonial Pact** to find out the truth. Africa does not plunder, does not steal the goods and wealth of France. But the African countries colonized until now by France pay annually fifty percent of their receipts to France, in the French Treasury, in an account called operating account (colonial taxes ?!). France has the exclusive right to plunder natural resources, mining, raw materials, all African wealth for centuries. Let's read the **Code Noir** to find out the social, economic, political, spiritual, cultural, human, physical harm that France, England, Holland, Belgium, Spain, Portugal and others have caused to Africans. Europe has always denied humanity, culture, civilization to Blacks. Mr Nicolas Sarkozi, ex-President of France, said that Africa has not made enough history. This speech is very pure racism in the manner of Hegel, Voltaire, Gobineau, Levy-Bruhl, Montesquieu, the Bible (Cham). It is again he who affirms loud and clear that Africa is too populated and that this represents a great danger for the global ecological and economic balance. Thus the kings and the French presidents are at the base of the danger of corona virus against Africa. They are still working for the destruction of Africa, for the extermination of Africans, for the depopulation of Africa. "Africa delenda est" (Africa must be destroyed or we must destroy Africa). We are still at the time of the Punic wars when the Roman conquerors said: "Carthago delenda est" (Carthage must be destroyed or else we destroy Carthage). And they did destroy Carthage. These are the consequences and manifestations of European racism against Africa. Corona virus is intended for the suppression of Africans, for the depopulation of Africa.

Experimenting corona virus in them and killing some of their compatriots with this virulent poison, Westerners distract, deceive and manipulate humanity. They are too cunning. They thus give themselves the necessary alibi and the right to wage their war of extermination of Africans and arbitrary occupation of Africa. They make up machiavellian, skillfully, their barbarism, their cynicism, their imperialism and their slavery practice. This is the cunning of art capitalized thy slave s. They give some small strokes themselves then they i RONT legitimately decimate all Africans. President Macron's speech ("We are at war ...") clearly means: Africa must be destroyed by all means, by a weapon invisible to the naked eye, by a chemical, biological, physical poison. This poison is called the corona virus (covid-19). "Africa delenda est" so that the French and their associates and accomplices can live better on earth. Good to hear, hi! We have been warned. A wise man is worth two, they say.

SECOND PART

THE SOCIO-POLITICAL ORIGIN OF CORONA VIRUS

"We are at war"

Emmanuel Macron

France is at war with whom? How? Why?
With what intentions?
For what purposes?

1

SLAVERY

The misfortunes, sufferings and massacres of Africans began with the policies of the Western kings and presidents. We can review the odious, despicable, barbaric, immoral and criminal acts of Westerners: the Black Code, slavery, colonialism, the Charter of Imperialism, the Colonial Pact ... The depopulation of Africa has started with the slave trade (slavery). This consisted of deporting 400,000,000 Africans to the Americas and Europe. The Arabs have done the same or more. Thus Blacks have always been used as instruments and beasts of burden to build, develop and enrich the countries of the whites and the Arab countries. Africans are the arms, heads, machines, tools of Westerners and Arabs. They gave everything to Europe, to America and to East: their blood, their flesh, their energy, their work force, their goods, their wealth, their cultural and civilizational values. Thanks to slavery and the slave trade, Africans are present everywhere, on all continents. They work for everyone, create, invent and produce goods, wealth and values of all kinds. Humanity and its values are their works. They are the founding fathers of the world, the engine of history, the cradle of humanity.

But all these blessings from Africans are wickedly, jealously and dishonestly concealed, stolen and denied by whites and Arabs. These two peoples have engaged in a balance of power, from dominator to dominated, from master to slave with their ancestors which are Africans. Abuse and endless atrocities are the weapons used by whites and Arabs in this race struggle. Corona virus crowns and perfects their weapons of mass destruction against Africans. They announce, predict that millions of Africans will perish by their act, that is to say by corona virus. They say it out loud, without moral scruples, bluntly, without the slightest shame, on TV, radio and social media. Corona virus is the perfect substitute for the atomic bomb and the nuclear bomb. It will cause genocide, slaughter and holocaust in Africa. Africa will become Nagazaki and Hiroshima. In the name of hatred, slavery, racism, capitalism and imperialism. The spirit of evil or the spirit of slavery has stuck to the skin of Westerners and Orientals (Arabs and Chinese). They cannot get rid of it. This is their Siamese brother, their quid proprium, their ipseity, their substance or essence.

2

COLONIALISM-NEOCOLONIALISM

"We are at war," French President Emmanuel Macron said. He added: "The enemy is invisible". Let's just say that the weapon used in this war is invisible to the naked eye. It is called corona virus. It was made by Westerners and Asians. It is intended to kill very massively and to drastically reduce the world population and mainly that of Africa. Because the African population (2 billions) is considered too large. France has thus openly entered into a genocidal war against Africa. At the historic Berlin conference (1884-1885), predatory Europeans shared the African continent like a big cake. They have made themselves masters and owners of Africa. France and England have carved out lion's share. It's called the colonization of Africa. It is the refined, diluted form of slavery (the slave trade). The African peoples colonized by France are in a way slaves of France. They are subjected to the will of France. They are "drudgery and cut to thank you". They do not have the right to rule themselves (they are directed) nor to produce economic goods, wealth for themselves. They were subjected to forced labor and locked up in gigantic open-air prisons, very well controlled, supervised and managed by France (whose national motto is however: Liberty, Equality, Fraternity). They are **French colonies**.

From 1960, these colonial territories became nominally independent. They are now governed indirectly by France because Africans have replaced the Whites at the head of these colonies. They manage affairs according to the orders, rules and laws of France and in the interest of France. This machiavellian system is called neo-colonialism or **Françafrique** (from Charles de Gaulle to this day). Its charter is the **Colonial Pact.** This legal act, which links France to its so-called ex-colonies, is the real source of corona virus. It is the greatest danger there is. It has always ravaged fourteen African countries. It does too much damage and casualties. It monstrously enriches France, a great eternal parasite, too greedy, shameless and cynical. The Colonial Pact impoverishes and destroys Africa. Thus the CFA-ECO franc, French military bases, terrorism, armed rebellions, coups d'Etat, war everywhere, the assassinations of rebellious African leaders, worthy, responsible, resistant, patriots, Pan-Africanists, sovereignists, independentists and revolutionaries like Sekou Touré, Modibo Kéita, Thomas Sankara, Sylvanus Olympio, Mouamar Kadhafi, Patrice Lumumba, Kwame Nkrumah, Amilcar Cabral...

Corona virus is from neocolonialism. It is a neo-colonial act against Africa. This is Françafrique at its peak as a criminal conspiracy in financial, economic, political, social and military matters. It is a system or a method of predation, of raiding on a global scale through the depopulation of Africa. It is a planetary catastrophe.

3

GLOBALIZATION - COLONIZATION

The program called globalization is underway. What is the meaning of globalization? What is the goal of globalization? Who is globalizing? Who is globalized? What do we gain from globalization? Should we accept globalization? Who rules the world?

Globalization is a subversive action of order. It is the attempt to abolish the world civilization. It is the very violent change of the world wanted by a group of very reckless, cynical, barbarian individuals, Luciferians, Freemasons, Illuminati who rule the earth. Globalization is the greatest danger today against the lives of all, against the population and civilization of the world. Globalizers have a political plan, an economic plan, a social plan, a security plan, a health plan, a military plan, a technological-scientific plan, a spiritual or religious plan.

At the political level, the globalizers want to impose a world government, dynastic, ultra-capitalist for their benefit. They will enslave all the weak in the world. Economically, this government will set very strict market and trade rules.

It will have the monopoly on all economic activities (agro-food, industries and others). It will decide everything and regulate world economic life. It will manage and control all the goods and all the riches of the earth with a standoff. At the social level, the world government will invent new living and working conditions for all earthlings, a new way of organizing work that will replace human work with machine work (robots) thanks to the internet. Everything will now be done remotely thanks to computers. It will be the triumph of technology (machinery). School will no longer have the right to classrooms where students are brought together to train, instruct and educate them. Classrooms will be replaced by computers and cell phones (smart phones). The courses will be given to the learners through the mediation of the internet. Computing alone will do all the work and solve all of life's problems. Medical care will also be given to the sick remotely. There will be no more interpersonal contact because the machines will do everything for men and will serve them as intermediaries, mediators. All services and public works will be automated. There will be surveillance cameras everywhere and electronic monitoring chips in every individual's body. This will be the guarantee of universal security. No more policeman as a human and physical person. Each individual will be fed, housed, cared for, educated and maintained free of charge by the world government. All their needs will be met free of charge and remotely. A census of the world population will be made for this purpose thanks to the electronic chip present in the body of each one. There will be very few people (20 percent of the current world population) to support, feed, care for, house, educate etc. thanks to the planetary genocide, to the reduction of the world population.

Demographics and the birth rate around the world will be brought under control. There will be the sterilization of most of the women and the killing of children, the elderly and the aged with poisoned vaccines. For this purpose, corona virus is created. Other poisons already exist and will also be used. Globalization is a soft war with silent weapons. It is a question of remaking the world, of founding a new civilization thanks to the triumphant science and technology of today. So science and technology will henceforth be omnipresent in the daily life of humanity. Scientists and technicians will take the place of God. They will hold the life and destiny of all in their hands. They will have the right to life and death over all humans. They will create humans by artificial methods: cloning, insemination. They are going to practice eugenics. It will be the triumph of robotics.

4

THE TERRORISM OF GLOBALIZING POWERS

Terrorism is the political method of using terror to achieve its end. Terrorists usually proceed by bombardments, attacks, assassinations and kidnappings. Terrorism is "a system of systematic violence to which certain extremist political movements have recourse to create a climate of insecurity favoring their designs" (Charles Debbasch, **Lexique de termes politiques**). Any member of a political organization that uses violence is a terrorist. Terrorist violence manifests itself in different ways: sabotage, hostage-taking, killings, destruction of public buildings with explosives, etc. Terrorism is a modern and universal weapon or political instrument. It is for the use of both the powerful-dominators and the weak-dominated. But it has its deep roots in Western history and civilization, especially in France.

Originally, "Terrorism was a government by terror that was in effect in France during the revolutionary period. Terrorism was the regime of Terror, that is to say that it dates from the period of the French Revolution from September 1793 to July 1794. We sometimes also call the First Terror, the period extending from 10 August to September 20, 1792 between the capture of the Tuileries and the first meeting of the Convention. It's a very dirty French story. This historical situation of terrorism and Terror clearly shows that the European civilization which was exported, transplanted to America (by means of colonization) is based on violence, terror and barbarism. Is there greater terrorism (or savagery) than the slave trade, colonialism and racial discrimination, neo-colonialism and all the genocidal wars that are raging everywhere and which have white people as common perpetrators? Which represent themselves, paradoxically, as GOOD, in their manichaean and narcissistic impetus, in their morbid self-glorification, in their complex of superiority, power, development. It is a question of bad faith on the part of a demon who thinks he is an angel or an executioner who takes himself for a victim. Who are we making fun of? **It must stop**. Can the Chinese claim or allege that it was Africans who created or spread corona virus in China? Let's stop this game of bad faith.

Terrorism is the work of whites and Asians. It is their past and their present. It is they who practice it on all the earth that they dominate and exploit happily, without any moral scruples, with cynicism and sadism. Corona virus is a terrorist attack carried out by Western and Asian powers. It is the present expression of capitalism, of globalization, of imperialism. It is a strategic means for re-slavery, recolonization of Africans and strengthening of white and Asian domination over the world. Who benefits from the depopulation of the earth? Who benefits from the current genocide (covid-19)? Who complains about the galloping African demographics?

5

NATURE AND VALUE OF HUMANITY

Humanity is made up of many different peoples. We can roughly distinguish between European peoples, African peoples and Asian peoples (simplification). Each of these peoples has its own characteristics or dominant traits. Let us focus here on moral traits (characters) only. Let's leave aside the physical and other traits. Let us look at the European peoples first. They are conquering, bellicose, predatory and barbarian peoples. They are vampires. They have filled human history with their endless crimes and their barbaric, violent and immoral acts. They wage war everywhere and against all other peoples. They attacked, invaded Africa, America, Asia, Oceania (expansionism). They committed genocides, massacres wherever they arrived. So they enslaved Africans for five centuries. Then they colonized them for two centuries (and this continues today under masks). They perpetrated the same crimes and the same barbarities in America against Native Americans. They are thieves, looters, brigands, killers. They have shaped and transformed Africa and America according to their interests and tastes. They transplanted their societal, cultural and civilizational models to Africa and America. They created unitary states and colonial nation-states there which they dominate and exploit on all levels. They have made themselves absolute masters and owners of Africa and America. They killed too many people there, caused too much misery, suffering and damage. And today, humanity is chained and buried by this criminal phenomenon of corona virus, an evil, apocalyptic earthquake.

In Asia, these same barbaric Europeans caused unforgettable pain and misfortune. They attacked the Vietnamese. They made war on them and tried to colonize them and enslave them. But it didn't work out well for them. They were defeated and pushed back by the Vietnamese, less armed and less equipped than them. They met a very valiant, very brave and very courageous people there. They succeeded in taking part of China, the island part (Formosa). They succeeded in taking part of Korea: South Korea. They reign over Japan which they bombed very cruelly and defeated during the Second World War. They colonized Malaysia, India etc. But the Hindus succeeded in freeing themselves from their domination thanks to the mortal struggle of the sage Mahatma Gandhi and his companions.

Asian peoples who are under the influence of Buddhism, Taoism and Hinduism are rather disciplined and wise. On the other hand, those who are dominated by Islam are violent, slavers. They have enslaved black people for centuries. They raided Africa. Arabs have nothing but contempt for Blacks. They never stop massacring them, humiliating them, mistreating them at home and everywhere. They are very racist and very cruel.

CORONA VIRUS

African peoples still suffer from domination, wickedness, contempt and boundless violence from Europeans and Asians. They forgive and tolerate everything. Out of weakness, ignorance, idiocy and cowardice. They are resigned, stoic. They only suffer the injustice and arbitrariness of barbarians and imperialist predators. They are disunited, divided, oppressed and exploited endlessly. They are very hospitable, peaceful, put to sleep by their animism which obliges them to always do good and never to do evil. The response to the crimes, injustices and arbitrariness of slavers and imperialists is forbidden to them by the Christianity imposed by predators. They are alienated, enslaved and dozing by all the colonialist and slave ideologies (their opium). So they accept the unacceptable. "If one strikes you on the left cheek, we must reach the right cheek". They are prohibited from cultivating the spirit of revenge and resentment against their torturers. They are thus forced into total, eternal submission, passivity, historical irresponsibility. All their political leaders are corrupt, alienated, controlled and directed by the imperialist-slavers. They are puppets, servants, guards of "prisons" or colonial enclosures. They are worse than their colonialist bosses and masters, slavers. They are resonance boxes, amplifiers and Trojans of Western-centricity. They are toxic waste or the worst corona virus.

CONCLUSION

The war for the globalization of all peoples is raging. Fundamental questions arise on this subject: does this war have any benefits? Does it have any misdeeds? Who among us will be lucky enough to survive this? What will be his fate? Will this fate be enviable or regrettable? Who really rules the world? How will the world be governed tomorrow? What if we democratize globalization?

We are witnessing the most atrocious and deadly war in history. The true **third** world war that dare not speak its name. Its purpose is to drastically reduce the population of the earth. **Only a handful of people** based in the West have decided it for all of humanity, illegitimately, arbitrarily. To make matters worse, it comes from those who call themselves democratic champions. It is not just and fair from the West which is the world's policemen and donors of moral lessons, which always make war on the Third World for not practice or imperfect practice of liberal democracy. Is the current globalization war a democratic action? For it to be a democratic action, it would have been necessary to proceed by a popular vote, by a world referendum, by consulting all the peoples of the earth. It would have been necessary to obtain the agreement of all humanity or a planetary consensus. But that was not the case at all. Dictatorially and unilaterally, a few powerful capitalists thirsty for human blood and inspired by lucifer have launched a bloody attack on all the inhabitants of the earth in order to eliminate all the weak by surprise. These include, in particular, the very famous Bill Gates, Bilderberg Club and many others as the executioners of everyone. In Africa, GSK's vaccine kills infants and children with impunity. There is no Pharmaco-vigilance to investigate crimes related to vaccinations and demand damages as it is done in Asia, especially in India and Pakistan. The rules of bio- ethics or e international ethics are violated cheerfully and with impunity by GSK. There 's no "consentement éclairé " in Africa. Understand the appeal or heart cry launched by Dr. Jerome Munyangi (Congolese researcher). "Let us take inspiration from the Indian model. We must bring GSK to justice. Let our children stop being used as guinea pigs in the laboratory. They are being killed since 2015 up today by the GSK vaccine, that is a biological weapon. Let us urgently create our Pharmaco-vigilance. We need independent and responsible scientists. The time has come to act to save African children ", he said.

Assuming that this cruel war is won by that band of scoundrels, how will the global village it wants to create be organized and governed? All of this is unknown at this moment. It's the devil's secret. Wait and see. Can the devil and the demon make mankind happy? Can they create a heaven on earth for everyone?

BOOK SUMMARY

This book is at the same time historical, philosophical, genealogical and prospective. It lays bare the corona virus plot. It is a breviary as a guide that demystifies genocidal globalization.

AUTHOR BIOGRAPHY

François Adja Assemien was born on March 15, 1954 in Ivory Coast. He studied classical literature (Latin and Greek), human sciences and philosophy. He holds a Ph D in Philosophy and a Bachelor's degree in sociology, and has devoted himself to the teaching of philosophy, writing and academic research. He is the author of several published works (novels, essays, short stories, plays). He works on his own concepts such as : Philocure, Afrocratism, Sidarology, Conscience Africaine, Phenomenologie de l'esprit et du comportement africain etc.

He speaks and writes three modern languages: English, French and German. He lives in the United States of America.

www.ingramcontent.com/pod-product-compliance
Lightning Source LLC
LaVergne TN
LVHW041550060526
838200LV00037B/1217